Thirst

First published in 1999 by
Slow Dancer Press
91 Yerbury Rd, London N19 4RW
England

British Library Cataloguing-in-Publication Data.
A catalogue record for this book is available from the British
Library.

ISBN 1 871033 50 0

Slow Dancer poetry titles are available in the U.K.
through Signature Book Representation distributed by
Littlehampton Book Services
and in the U.S.A. and Canada by Dufour Editions inc,
PO Box 7, Chester Springs, PA 19425 0007.

Cover Design: East Orange & Keenan
Cover Photography: Catherine Boudet

Printed by Bell and Bain, Glasgow

This book is set in Elegant Garamond 10.5/13

Slow Dancer Press

Thirst
Matthew Caley

Acknowledgments

Are due to the following periodicals: *Blade, Brando's Hat, The Bound Spiral, Dog, Poetry Durham, The Echo Room Yearbook, Foolscap, Lancaster Poetry Festival Anthology, London Magazine, Magma, The North, Orbis, Poetry London Newsletter, Poetry Review, The Rialto, Scratch, Slow Dancer, The Swansea Review, Tabla, Verse* and *The Wide Skirt* where some of these poems, or versions of them, were first published.

For Catherine

C'est dans ta coupe aussi que j'avais bu l'ivresse
Et dans l'eclair furtif de ton oeil souriant.
Gerard De Nerval

Contents

*'The imagination is like a drunk that has lost his watch
and has to get drunk again to find it'*

Guy Davenport
The Geography Of The Imagination

Freefall

John Berryman's Last Thoughts Written Somewhere
Between The Washington Avenue Bridge
and The Embankment

What a deep drop for Mistah Bones
and Co. Full fathom 5 Etc. A wave and here goes. Entrails
kerplonk quoth he
    and parachute-free completely. Fate bestrode.
Taking up the mantle - an heirloom suicide.
Some other bastard can be cross at God
while Randall, Ted and Delmore ride the midnight train
pulling out for limbo or Cape Cod.

Hail farewell elegant Daiquiri-girls on Buick bonnets,
a cream-cake, footloose, off the rails,
melted in her glove-compartment. Love failed.
    We were the nation's rioting corpuscles,
sick, sick, an epidemic,
one screw loose like a thirteen line sonnet.
O to meet Old Shakey on the golden shore. Icarus, smelted.
Much Ado About _____, all birds fly up.

All that water just to die of thirst. Hot-tot.
Plucky Sylv's third time lucky. Gas-green silk billow.
That shit Cal'll do a rollicking Obit. Boost book-sales.
    King Bear. Let him have it!
Wind-sock whoosh. Aerosol, arsehole...
wheee...Ferris wheel, will
Henry or me
hit the water first? Shit, missed it.

Thirst

Had licked the tyres of fifteen Topanga Canyon hot-rods
    and crawled into the watering-hole
where the first thing he sees is a delicate bubble,

adrift, liquid-languid, with all its glazes, its rainbow-oil windows
    and the barmaid, eleven layers of beauty on a roll
saying huskily 'Isn't it pretty?'. In reply he prods

it with the toe of his steel-capped cowboy boot and makes it burst.
    The softest plip followed by aftermath 'Oh's'.
He instantly forgets the woman he loves. Orders a double. Thirst.

Franco's

Where I am enclaved
wasting this Holy Thursday
devouring Ian Gibson's *Lorca*,
a pasta-twirl
or a
Parma-ham pizza
with its ripe, polished olive at the centre of everything.

EVERYONE KNOWS
PINCUS ROSE
FOR SMARTEST CLOTHES

Ian Gibson? Pincus Rose? Lorca?
Who decides on the name of a gas
or The Sea Of Tranquillity?

His voice is so deep it provided the lining for his shoes.

*

Where else could one discuss
rare groove,
the etymology of 'by Jove'
or the prose-style of *Contre Sainte-Beuve*
with the waiter's face and jacket as white as coral?

I am wondering if he will guess the name
of the man in the 'loose author's tie'
who defied authorities' noose
and found his own Gethsemane
in an olive-grove

when a Rasta-girl
breaks from the impatient queue with a view to
my pizza's black-hole, my cappucino's Saturn-ring.

'Do you mind if I step into your grave?'

Bespoke Tailors

Of which not much has been heard
this particular decade, unlike alluvial rain
which makes all the headlines with ease.
The night is full of loss-adjusters on the prowl,
mating felines and members of the Neighbourhood Watch
Scheme, who, during the day, are butchers, bespoke tailors

Etc. Gumball machines are as rare as bespoke tailors
these days, picked up by herds
of market-traders at car-boot sales who watch
out for bargains and any hint of rain
on their way home across playing fields where prowl
-ers might rob them with particular ease.

Parents feel worried about their kids being sold E's
by strange gentlemen with the manners of bespoke tailors
who strut along every cul-de-sac - no need to prowl.
One even deals from the church porch or so they've heard,
slipping the little packet into a palm undercover of alluvial rain
while the neighbourhood looks at its watch.

The kids from the neighbourhood watch
out to intercept their exam results, mostly D's and E's
and F's and 'See Me's'. Their parents have heard rumours
                              of the reign
of The Queen Mother when bespoke tailors
could be found on every street and the town crier was heard
egging on friendly coppers to chase away the prowlers.

No coppers now to see kids on the prowl,
nipping out the back window after *Neighbours* or *Crimewatch*
while their parents nod in assent as Douglas Hurd
parries difficult questions with the old-school ease
of men who get their coats taken in by bespoke tailors
and thus keep their necks dry under alluvial rain.

So days are spent calibrating the rain
-fall for any average November or on the prowl
for *Capstan* and *Senior Service*. The shop-signs of bespoke tailors
piled in skips for a bonfire the whole neighbourhood watches,
their lit-up faces betraying a sense of unease
as the names melt and crackle. Names once whispered

in polite circles will soon be unheard
of now that the stacked watch
-tower of the bonfire has crumbled with particular ease.

Blackout

I came to
through haloes of *Paracetamol*
between the splayed bodies
of two of The Three Fates. Their rows of *Penguin Classics*
in alphabetical order, their tacky spines, their musty odour.
At least two of our six legs
belonged to no-one.

I came to
on the fifth floor of a four-storey squat
in the bed of its absentee owner.
Bailiffs or a hangover were knocking at my skull.
My wrist-bracelet bore the legend - Neil Bymouth.
I was dressed
in a frock of organza and chenille.

I came to
outside of Troy, one of a cohort
of snoring soldiers. A campfire stuttered and went out.
Little girls played cricket. Someone projected the shadow
of a grazing horse on the side of a lit-up bell-tent.
I looked down at my watch
but I never wear one.

I came to
poleaxed and naked in a rhododendron glade
that turned to a Municipal flower-bed. I looked at the moon
which was five minutes slow. Its left hand stroked *The Sea Of Tranquillity*.
Who named *The Sea Of Tranquillity?* I have to know.
A rhododendron
is a bush with six equal sides.

I came to
in a hammock slung between certainty and doubt
next to *La Belle Dame Sans Merci*. A Red Admiral tattoo
just-healed about her paling shoulder blade.
It seemed piquant to mention that butterflies mate in mid-air.
But when I shuffled off for my shower
she sneaked out.

I came to
between my sleeping parents,
their pale, stringy bodies separate and afloat.
A phial of migraine pills on my father's side. A bible on my mother's.
I have lain between them for years like a double-edged sword.
I wanted to speak
but my mouth wouldn't utter a word.

I came to
in a chamber of air and light.
The back-lit veins in my eyeball were the veins of a floating leaf.
Apparently I was levitating fifteen
feet up in the air. One of Wim Wenders' angels nuzzled my ear.
'This isn't a near-death experience,
this is the after-life'.

I came to
in a hedge between two gardens
saying 'Pardon?' to no-one in particular. A cold bird burbled
in the sedge. My hair was stuck with scented nightstock, brambles,
nettles, deadly nightshade, myrtle. The horns of a hangover
were growing through my skull.
I stood up and went out to get mortal.

Drunks waking, see the sun

As something other than us. Emerging
        from underneath their hangovers
like lions from out of the shade
        they tumble out
into untold sunlight and dust. Like children
        they can either stay put
or totter. Lead weights hang

        in their heavy trees.
The day, the day that has begun
        without their permission
is as clear as heaven. They will
        look for a brink on which to teeter.
Sunlight is the enemy. Milkmen
        an extinct species.

So they lie on their backs like star
        -gazers considering dust. Dust,
I tell you, dust. Nothing has ever had
        quite the importance
of dust, bright algae of the eye, motes billowing
        up some sunshaft
in their billions. Drunks cry 'Dust!'

        and everyone answers.
Yesterday is a rumour started
        by dust. Drunks gingerly
open their mouths as if to the
        dentist and murmur
'Czechoslovakia, Czechoslovakia'. They have
        always lost at least two shoes.

Drunks waking, see the sun
    as something other than us. They
talk to their hats on long-distance phones.
    Midwives to themselves
they are born off doorsteps, plinths
    and hardening beds. Their heads
full of feathers, their pillows

    full of stones. There was a woman -
there must have been a woman. So far
    down the parched road
that her face is blurring, emerging
    wet, through the pillow
like The Lady Of Shalott. Basho had
    some haiku about this but

fuck it, they forget. Git. Drunks
    are startled by their own hands.
They know the sun is the mother
    of dust. How she kindles each speck
to dance, to glow. They tremble like dust
    in a curtain-chink or
wake up under trees, seeing them

    as vague gods, silvery
as the undersides of fish, calling them
    to where they cannot go. When what
they wish to know, too late,
    is why they are always sober
when the rest of the world is so drunk. Drunks waking
    see the sun then evaporate.

Bending Under The Laburnum

that overhangs the litter-filled alleyway that leads
    inevitably, to the scaffolded, Tulse Hill
towerblock where I live, for the one thousand
    -th time it has struck me,
low in the face like a whiplash, that this must be

    the one thousandth time
I have bent under this laburnum. Stooped even, under
    its hang-dog, pendulous flowers,
their pale-purple, up-ended chandeliers like
    the enormous earrings of a Diva

warbling The Queen Of The Night's solo
    from *The Magic Flute*. Yes, it has struck me,
that I have always stooped, night after night,
    before and after this laburnum, have never
stooped so low, in fact, avoiding the low

    -flying debris. No, never so low.
So I imagine, some future night, totally drunk,
    (why totally drunk, I cannot think)
that I don't stoop or bend but blunder
    gloriously, all my six foot three

and a half fully immersed and un-rehearsed
    in its overhanging flower-bath.
Mugged by fragrance, assailed by scent
    sharp as spleen or iodine
so my own head is a scented chandelier. It's

    as lush as some floral carwash.
All my windows burnished and lathered
    with petals, bee-stings, purple, gnats,
scented and full as the correspondence
    from Chopin to George Sand. No, next time

I will not stoop or bend
  to the litter-filled alleyway like the thin
reed in the parable but plunge ignominiously
  into purple to emerge
somewhere between Tulse Hill and Samarkand.

Sycamore, Sycamore

I am so high up in my sycamore that no-one else can follow.

dwindled
      Gawain
            wan on a tricycle
                  an overshadowed
shadow

I am so high up in my sycamore that no-one else can follow.

tipsy with wind
      Dandelion & Burdock
            burped, utterly un-usurped
                and her, the girl-usurper
down below

I am so high up in my sycamore that no-one else can follow.

a Stockbroker-belt
      of graveyards and garden centres
            at eye-level
                gnats and centaurs
tennis-nets lift and billow

I am so high up in my sycamore that no-one else can follow.

her at the tap-root
      softly encircling
            pleading, pleading
                Pirate At Forty
hair and hope receding, slow

I am so high up in my sycamore that no-one else can follow.

Bible Class

My hands make a spire, a rood-screen
then a congregation of fingers. God was annoyed
and lightning hit the weather-vane. They told us
each altar contained the bones of a saint,
-Lawrence, Chrozogonos, Cosmos and Damien -
their fingerknuckles buoyant in formaldehyde.

There are enough splinters from the One, True Cross
to build a clipper ship. But where would it sail?
The Holy Grail is a sort of seabird
that only flies in foggy conditions and Mary
had an apple in her belly. Eve ate it or the snake.
Did Jesus ever walk on Hyson Green?

Prince Charles and Moses talk to plants.
Once, I sipped from the holy water font
and shivered by cold marble, waiting for the whiskey-kick
of The Holy Ghost. His body is a mauve oval
that lives in the tabernacle. Does he own a fridge?
My fingers ache as a spire. I try a rabbit silhouette instead.

Mrs Fisher says the crucifixion was achieved by acupuncture.

Lent

During which I deprived myself of *Small Rich Tea*
and the statues were covered in purple plush.

Victimae Pascali Laudes in polyphonic tempo.
I was doubting Thomas without the saviour.

The shifty congregation tried to study
the vaulted ceiling's chiaroscuro arcs

and the organ took on a sonic hush
when an altar-boy's hair

spontaneously-combusted during Credo
only to be fanned out by the cool priest's

dovelike hands. He didn't miss a quaver.
Later, I watched two bishops drag their cassocks

through a gargoyled archway.
Their croziers like ornate question-marks.

?

In *The Lacemaker* by Vermeer
all the focal alignment
is trained upon a non-existent needle,
which paradoxically, does exist, purely because of context.

Dali, so we've heard,
decided it was composed of rhinoceros horns
which became the constituent component
of his *St John Of The Cross*.
He would wake most days
and defecate
a rhinoceros-horn-shaped turd.
Of course, it was just a phase.

*

Over the mystery of the airwaves
we heard a tardy chancellor
herald with glee the latest unemployment figures.
A problem solved is a problem ___
for the dressmaker who drew blood with a sliver of air.

*

So we wonder if similar problems are involved
in the worship of the moon-goddess Isis,
the man who can part clouds by telekinesis
or The Holy Mass?
Let's sew it all up in a huge, doctoral thesis

for the girl who has not left that I already miss.

Onanist

This green, bilious
bell-tent of a duvet.
Insidious alarm-tick. Her head-dent in the pillow.
Two days unshaved. The low whiff of her sea-scent.
He pummels his prick, that single, solitary act
and grades the various darks.

Poets are the biggest wankers
with their imaginations well-equipped
to enlarge upon the erotic:
the way a T-shirt interacts with its wearer,
her breasts so earlobe-soft, the cool waft
on his leg as she turns a page of the latest Milan Kundera...

all grist, all grist to the mill.
The boyish small of her back
like a pebble in a brook.
Peeling skin from mushroom-mauvish glans,
he pictures her - The Nameless, Faceless One- undressed.
A shingle-thrash. A rash of minnowed sparks.

He comes. Then feels depressed.

Fenugreek

Two Sag Aloos gone from their tin-foil trays.
I lay on
his hard futon
as if it were a raft of water lillies

like some supine voluptuary.
I loved him then
with the fierce love that Jesus had
for Mary and Martha, Martha and Mary

watching him sip the dark nectar.
After, a *Black Cat* dwindled ash into the ether
but when he padded out, pale and un-pyjamma'd

to take a leak
I wondered if he could tell that my armpits sang
not with the stink of love but fenugreek, pure fenugreek.

How To Sleep With A Woman

Take to the streets under neon, Pleiades or Plough,
find a house, any house,
that broken drainpipe, gnarled tree or trellis
then ascend and enter through

the conveniently
-open window. Adjust to the lack of light,
wrestle out of your shirt.
Let down your underclothes, slide gently under

the cool sheets next to her.
She'll be adrift from her moorings on your starboard side.
Inhale that undersheet smell of body-warmth and *Dreft*.
The curled leaf of her hand, the dividing line of her behind-

touch only with the fingertips of the mind.
Now she is laid out for you like a burial mound,
might call out a name - John, *Paracetamol*, Honey-Love-
but do not move-one might be yours-but do not move,

rather tune-in to the orchestral gurglings of the large intestine,
that one, sly, sweet fart, all the wonderful machinery
at work. Or count each freckle, each follicle
speckling the pillow. If her blood is tugged by the moon

and she blushes and howls like a wolverine
we will allow
you to cool her troubled brow
with your breath. But her peeping breast, her sleeping crotch

must not be attempted. Stay true to your stilly vigil. Your
                              nightwatch.
Lie still and parallel like rafts upon the water
until dawn, that other laggard, sidles under the door.
Do not doze -please- do not doze. Wake and leave before she does.

Theme And Variation

All the flats
    I've ever lived in
had ceilings that leaked
    or walls unravelled by condensation.
They were temporary
    as tents.
God wouldn't separate me
    from the elements.

He continued to send
    lovers to drive me up the wall.
One arm snared
    in unravelling tresses
('Tresses?'- 'Hair'.) The other losing sensation
    inside swirling, paper-thin dresses.
They were temporary, too.
    A brief inhalation of passing scents.

One landlord was
    'God's gift to women'
and drilled a secret peephole in the wall
    to catch them, Degas-like,
rising from the bath
    or going to take a leak.
His eye the eye of a spy
    receiving leaked memos from The Government.

I yearned for pristine isolation
    like some temporary God
or little icy star
    yet lived within paper-thin walls
beset by lover's wails
    leaking through the wallpaper.
Thereafter, laughter
    or arguments.

While my ceiling swirled
    I heard them
invoking deities
    on the edge of extremis-
'Oh my God, my God"
    as if temporarily
pushed beyond their bodies
    they had blent,

then unravelled through walls of light to another world.

Three Part Harmony

They are fucking in the bath. Turned
away from him, her knuckles on the taps
burn white as snowdrops.
A spawn-cluster of *Radox* bubbles escape
onto the tiles. He slaps
more urgently against her suddy cheeks.

Tip-toe on the topmost rung the window
-cleaner's eyes strain the addled glass.
His mouth delineates half-formed words.
Part of him goes so deep inside of her
that when she cries the sound comes from his mouth.
Tile-echo. Tap-gurgle. Froth.

The window cleaner shifts his footing, checks,
slips on his chamois leather, falls backwards, arms out wide-
the bollards below him tiny as snowdrops.
All three cry simultaneously.
The cry of a man that sounds like the cry of a woman.
The cry of a bird.

Vigilance

Wild Bill Hickock
would never offer
the back of his head to an open doorway -

Spring, progress, Prohibition, the dustbowl's sway,
love or fear,
The Wild West's first car -

all could enter
the aperture.
Whilst the slightest click

or breeze upon his nape-fur
might mean endless light
inside his head forever.

This Once Great Ladies-Man

now cut back operations to the bone
    or, in business-jargon, rationalised his output.
Put phallus in mothballs,
    metaphorically, became

less like a modern-day Satyr
    and more like a much-distanced arbiter
of taste, as it were,
    off-limits to himself below the waist.

As with all ex-Casanovas
    and De Sades
this change was a passionate change
    -no half-measures or pressures could impinge.

Old flames were neither re-kindled or courted
    meaning slightly less than the sparks
from his cowboy boots on the courtyards
    and watering-holes

that he hardly now frequented. His velvet cushions,
    embroidered with so many snatch-impressions
kept gathering dust. His vellum-bound volumes
    containing *Polaroids* of dozens

of clitori like so many pinned and atrophied
    butterflies went likewise. Through endless practice
abstinence became as strong a thirst as lust. There
    were so many notches on his bedpost

it was whittled to a brittle
    wand - an antenna whose slightest waver
-ings spoke of coiled haunches
    and powdered crotches - and then to sawdust. Thus, bit by bit,

this man who could elicit
    a pre-coital moan from the moon
or even the coldest stone of a Rodin seemed able
    to define himself by less, more lyric

than epic. His tongue might envelope an earlobe,
    his mind breathe in the musky,
freckled skin of some half-sleeping non-conquest
    or linger on the pale-purple aureola

of some slacker or star-child's breast
    as her E's or whatever wore off
but nothing that broached the physical. Thus caps, coils and pills
    were no impediment. No need

for duels with pearl-handled pistols,
    blunt instruments or fencing-foils,
no listing the personal details in his Database
    Of Girls, just perfume-wafts and after-traces,

the trickle of sweat down a swaying spine
    mingled maybe with patchouli-oil
he could catalogue and define at fifty paces.
    It should be stated that this change

was nothing to do with phases of the moon,
    some vague, post-Feminist, or, Lord God, New Man
revisionism, nothing to do with age (he was three years
    younger than Don Juan at a similar stage

and ahead, fifteen to one, in fact
    in pure terms of actual numbers fucked)
nor with the proliferation
    of exotic and not-so-exotic diseases,

nor with that most common of causes
     'the love of a good woman' but more
with - with the splitting of the atom,
     of no longer seeing this one or that one

as single entities but more
     of a plural phenomenon
made up of endless, little sensations, the many in the one,
     which made for a concentrated kind of bliss

which bordered, dare I say it, on the religious.
     He had settled, at last, settled
like dust, for less. And thus, as ingenues and lushes
     mourned the loss,

this once-great ladies man
     made peace with the last few Gods
that he could easily believe in
     and eased his passage into Hades.

Love Poem : Final Demand

So, Where is it then?
The heartfelt work that incontestably prove
-s your actual feelings for me, or your love,
whichever phrase comes close.

You say that it's a matter of ill-luck, some strange malaise,
blame it on writer's block,
lack
of a chaise-longue or inspiration. Lack of inspiration?

Look at the reams of stuff that Aragon
wrote for Elsa.
Shakespeare for The Dark Lady Of The Sonnets.
And you? Not a jot, a blip, a couplet or a haiku.

Trouble is you're arrogant,
so high up your own sycamore that you never look elsewhere.
But I'm no prop, no part-time Muse.
So fuck you,

Jacko.
Have it on my desk by 10.00 a.m tomorrow
or the deal's off. At least two pages long. Handwritten.
Oh yes, and sign it.

Aloof

Rather than a louche affair
with Lady Otteline Morrell-
this bag of salt and vinegar
crisps; this pint; this game of pool.

Eight Ways Of Looking At Lakes

1

From afar, like Ishtar, aloof
on some spectacular limestone outcrop,
though binoculars. You'll be suffering from a headache
beyond the reach of *Aspirin*. It is a headache-coloured sky
and the lake itself is a grey headache, an undistinguished lozenge,
part of a panoramic, cinemascopic sweep,
but boring beneath the sky's distemper,
small.

2

Imagine yourself a minor Lakeland poet,
far from his sister's tussock, plucking an albatross, nursing the itch
of syphilis. With his laudanum-phial and, of course,
his vellum-bound volume of verse. Things can only
get better after this.
Or worse.

3

Close-up. In sunshine. With everything holiday-brochure bright,
airbrushed even. Even. Catch the surface-spangles, gyres, spirals,
silvery ring-pulls, rivets, all chainmail-linked and glinting. Think
of the importance of surfaces. The planes of people's faces.
Be satisfied with shallows. Here clouds are mountains,
mountains clouds and sheeted lakes, inscrutable, mirror both.
For the adventurous, dip your toe halfway
up your toenail. For the gifted - get walking.

4*a*

Read W. H. Auden's *Lakes* [from *Bucolics*] and know all there is to know.
Almost. When you have finished, check the Ordinance Survey Map
of his face. Find solace in each fissure. Wallow.

4*b*

An ankle-deep paddle. We are 70% water ourselves. Little lopsided
waking lakes. Hardly amniotic. Hardly baptismal. Though
                            watch out
for suddenly sepulchral doves that come and go
in a tin-flash. And don't forget your socks
busy sunbathing on the bank.

5

Skinny-dipping. Let the salt support you. Think how many salt tears
would constitute a lake. That cold gasp as lakewater hits your groin.
Dippings, siftings, bits floating off. Your umbilical now knotted
and not in service. Sun-spangles on your cellulite
and your runny, foreshortened legs, thalidomide in rivulets.
Drift off, a jungle-raft to Samarkand and

6

have sex like waterbabies spawning in the spray.
The more professional can water-ski or analyse the wave-raked silt
replete with collective guilt and plastic goggles. Find the greeny-blue
bodies of underage boys and girls barely recognisable
from the local Echo or Star. Lapping darkness. The moiré effect
                            of bubbles.
Deep, deep. You are diving too deep.

7

The one rule is 'everything ends'.
You now have a choice between the bottom or the bends.

8

This is the bottom. Grey-blue, billowing. Krakens, crud.
Long-missed Masons, rust. An underwater city of muffled bells
malingering beyond. Water or land. No-one can tell which is which.
When you finally set foot in Atlantis
its dust is dry to the touch.

Ellsworth Kelly : Orange Red Relief

If you are going to die, and you are going to die, die
on a slatted bench at the Ellsworth Kelly exhibition
where his flat forms belly like sails, like sails
bent by stillness but containing movement
like a single, held note when the sound carries,
carries and dies.

You might die falling in love with *Orange Red Relief*,
falling in love with another man's wife, Sweet Delphine
in Room No 9. Where so much is suggested by the curve
                    of a line
that the heart drops but is held aloft by coolness.
Divorce Jack Youngerman
from such a clash of colour

and he would die, die in the Bois de Boulogne
while you waded in light. Or follow that woman
down 52nd Street and note in your pad the colours
of her scarf, the way they intersect each other, the way
Central Park sits like a green scarf
dropped on a snowy but thawing New York

by a madman hurrying to his loft. If you are going to die,
sail on the curve of that horizon as described by
distinguished historian Simon Shamen - *both rooted on*
                    the ground
and headed for heaven - and know that,
for once, a critic might well be right. Take your life there.
Have your skull trepanned by a huge slice of light.

Willem De Kooning : Pirate 1983

Douglas Fairbanks Senior
inveigled his cutlass into the giant canvas
sailed down the huge slit
to the deck-rails
and as soon as he landed, he leapt.

Love is followed by uncertainty
as surely as the hangover
follows the drinking spree.

*

The child who sailed
a horizontal stepladder
with its cargo of fake-gold and ghee
is lost at sea, for hours, will not be stilled.

His cargo of pungent oils
and flaming scarves
culled from nomadic tents or distant wharves.

That grandiloquent blister where the paint wept.

*

We will all arrive at Louse Point
to watch the light die, sporadically.

Similarly, when a kingfisher dives
its colours follow behind a fraction later
but catch up when it hits the water.
Then they wash off, like dyes.

*

Somewhere beyond the town
a figure in blue overalls
is watching white noise with the sound turned down.

White Noise

T'was in *White Noise* by Don DeLillo
    I found the faded leaf,
maple or oak, oak or maple, whichever way a leitmotif
    of that one, hot summer with her -
tousle-haired embezzler or stand-in Jeanne Duval,
    Miss Lemur or whichever pseudonym
might best befit her, gammy-legged sitter
    for Manet, de-camped to Brixton for a spell
and me the one to go under. That leaf was plucked from
    a low-slung oak the night we were locked
inside the wrought-iron gates of Brock
    -well Park, its dark

colon, low-slung oaks, her low-slung halter
    and halting, 'Let's do it here...'.
And so we did, against the backfire/shotgun sound
    -track and dog-bark : my perfect metre,
her feather-boa sprightly as a firework. It peters out...
    then all comes back, the girl
who gave the slip to each biographer. And now me too...
    My hooped, pale arms all
hooped on nothing but a hangover ...white noise
    of feathers crackling in the pillow,
white noise of *Alka-Seltzer* in a glass.
    A4 white noise. *White Noise* by Don DeLillo.

The Worm In The Bottom Of The Mescal Bottle
Has His Say

'Drain me down. Drain to the dregs of yourself.
I was born, not asked, to crawl into this world,
entered as a slimy carapace, ended up
pickled in limitless knowledge. Pour fire down your throat.
Let it rise like bilge in a leaky boat.
Here's sea-salt like stale tears. Here's bitter lemon.
Wait until your world starts to slide
like an ashtray on an incline.
Before the slither of drainpipes, before
    the knocking of bailiffs...

Let a world open up to you : *lush cacti choked*
by osmosis. The hacienda still stained by Malcolm Lowry's blood,
chilli-peppers rusting. Cortez's breastplate taking the full tilt
of the sun, plumes from steamy fumaroles and her,
nipple-deep in Spring and wading out to you
of her own, fierce, free will...
all forseen and germinated by me, this spineless shrimp.
Hold your glass clear up to the light bulb.
Drain it down. Plumb the bottom of the well.
    Then eat me and shine....'

Silvery

Hello, or for the connoisseur, *bonjour.*
My name's Kiki,
the demi-mondaine from Montparnasse.
Now up with The Olympians
or skiing down its phosphorescent,
fibre-optic grass
with the other animals
-ie artists, on my arse.
I jumped from beds to *bons mots,*
the appendixes of hefty encyclopedias.
He's still crowing about getting
the jump on The Vortographs,
thinking immortality
makes him less dead than me.
He likes my plump mind.
A draught-whisper of sciatica
howls through these F-holes
on my back.
Who's knelt between
Ingre's knees?

But being a cello has its moments.
Where once I had
half the Latin Quarter
- is that a third ? -
squawking inside my corsets,
now I rise like a luminous pear
from coffee-table art books.
I'm silvery as light on an eel.
But The Great Man
finds being vapour difficult.
Up here where
clouds stack themselves endlessly
shelf by shelf
he still comes shamelessly

whining for croissants
or the deep bass-twang
of my behind, hiding
all that brittle artistry
from the tumult that is himself.
Me? I'm silvery.

Here And There

i.m The Goncourt Brothers

Where
Edmond De Goncourt stands
with his quintessential lily-white hands
resting on the shoulder
-s of his non-existent brother

and elegantly
inscribes, with dutiful *de rigueur*
- two parts irony and two-parts ennui -
a flowery
in memorium of his shade.

They shared
ideas, *le journal*, underclothes, loves,
plus a profound distaste for Baudelaire's
slightly shop-soiled gloves,

but now it is all one side
-ed. They would walk
into L'Ecole Des Beaux Arts entirely naked
to get to the truth -

the bloom of a twisted rose, the bloom of youth.

Critical opinion hardens.

Their
greatest work
-s derided.

*

Three spoonfuls of potassium-bromide
in the Tuilerie Gardens -
having the nerve
to bitch
about Sainte-Beuve (having the itch.)

Given the urge they could be an ur-Gilbert and George.

*

First C's and T's
elude him.
His coiffure
reduced to a single hair.
Like Vaucorbeil he becomes afraid of sofas
(especially if they are velvet)
and squawks
at his own shadow.
Then absence begins to suit him to a T.
A lack of self.

Perpetuity.

Is the mirror his brother or his brother the mirror?

Out of habit they still share
the odd *bon mot*, idea, rhyme,
- light, frail light, to earth from a long-dead star -
that final entry,
a single letter,
the gulf between here and there.

Lord Hanson, Reclining

Grandfather started it in 1848. When, a century later,
    they nationalised his sweat,
I sailed off in disgust for the U.S.A, thinking
    I'd given Dear Old Blighty the chop.
But that was before M'Lady. The Goddess of blue rinse
    and silk-clad axe assumed the throne.
So I came back, replete with wife and contacts.
    Everything and everyone can be bought.
Imagine the highest number in existence, then add
    another naught. Regrets are solid bonds.
They increase in value year by year. I missed out on
    Audrey Hepburn just when I thought
I had her by the hair. I would have bought each one upon
    her ballerina head. They say
she was my first love. That was never so. It was
    a fishing and edible oils concern
in The Gulf Of Mexico.

    Paradise is an anaemic blast
of James Last and his supermarket strings.
    My radio station, *Melody*,
I created because of the inanity of D.J's at The BBC.
    Its signature tune is *Tenderly*.
It soothes my hardening arteries when The Gold Standard
    takes a beating. The sweat of miners
gargling inside my central heating. Frank will croon
    My Way at my funeral - a croaky,
be-wigged In Memoriam. A sort of proud apology
    for when they freeze my blood inside
a private crematorium. But I am too expensive.
    I'll never burn. The Dow Jones Index
will hold its breath until my return. I will acquire
    shares in Purgatory after I'm dead.
I can be quick as sunlight (courtesy of *Powergen*),
    slow as hair retreating from a forehead.

Marianne Moore : Desire's Overweening Ambition

Can be seen in Titian
      for instance
or those over-muscled quarterback Michelangelo gods
      lounging on clouds
as if they were chaise-longue.
      Or, from a suitable distance
the detached observer may achieve
      a cathedral-steeple
      out-reaching the tallest of trees
      where, up-ending

their paler bellies
      to the wind
the burgundy-coloured beech leaves utter something
      almost intelligible
as speech. Of course, appearances
      tend to deceive:
the fieldmouse has it - something
      of a striped tiger
      at dandelion-scale, the pale thwack
      of a Yankee batter

hauling aloft a long
      -shot, maybe,
beyond-stadium-bound, that up-stretching neck
      and bobbing Adam's apple
stationed at the mound. The blood
      lust of a bloodhound. The
Economic pamphleteering of my old
      friend Ezra Pound - moribund,
moribund. A slow snail negotiating
      lawns. As for love

no-one would quaver
          at her mousey
tirades: house-rules are for housemaids. Death did me
          no favour. Temperance craves
what temperance scorns - The God Of Love
                    is a god of horns. So give me
the tremulous quiver of cupid's
          arrow [but tipped by
tribesmen in curare], so, through
                    chalices of alchemic

wine I can sense your
          faux-Joan Of Arc
unarmoured by amour, and as chainmail's glints and
          gyres spiral to the floor
St Sebastianne can be adored as an immor
          -tal porcupine. My body isn't
mine. Merely some combustion of
                    ether and light.
          There is no bliss in proving one's
                    own thesis : I cannot write.

Great Writer Retired

He lets it go-
the monster in him shrinks
to palatable proportions.
Stipends from beneficiaries
and the odd chat-show
keep him in woollen socks.
He sits in a wheelchair
before a disciple
discussing Thoreau's pamphlet
-*The Necessity For Civil Disobedience.*
[Apparently he
never paid his Poll Tax
and was jailed six times].
Petrarch is anaemic.
Socrates the ugliest man in Athens.
Hangers-on swallow joss-sticks
in the garden
while he dozes lightly in a hammock
slung between belief and atheism
two pale oaks whose branches meet at the top.

Thorazine wings him to God.
Hair and patience thins.
He knows the only certainty
is doubt, all his frail pages
waiting on the verdict
of Judge Posthumous and Judge Hindsight.
Governments ban or knight him.
Ex-lovers sue or write books.
He reads Zukofsky's "A"
as meaning *anteater, avatar, alcohol.*
That naiad with personal stereo and no T-shirt
pales before recollection
of his Panamanian muse. Nevertheless

he divorces loyalty
and marries the silver birch. Bitch.
Follow now the dwindling light
to the dark interior
of his study - see its books face down
with broken spines, him shrinking
as the monster lets it go.

So, Fuck Off, Please

After Ezra Pound's Translation
Of Sophocles' Women Of Trachae

Translation is the art
of mishearing one word for another.
All the great translators
sat on their master's knees and gulped a glass of water
whilst simultaneously clacking their jaws.
Never have truck with such an avatar.

Into the dust they all go.

Cutie nicked all the prizes.
She's poison, piss and poison
but no-one else is such a shaker,
a mover and a shaker, yet unshaken.
We all know we're beneath her.
Yet no-one has the right to give her away.

Into the dust they all go.

Imagine. Two E-heads bust up over a babe-
all spittle and angel-dust,
rivers of it... bike-horns honking
like obdurate bulls in Pamplona.
At the end of their tether,
lashing and broody.

Into the dust they all go.

They twang car ariels
outside The Paradise Club
and Fracas, his pina-colada spiked
believes he's The Son Of God.
Legless under a Thunderbird duvet, Cutie's a fallen bride
eyeing a dowsing-rod.

Into the dust they all go.

Landlord

So, once more
you're

at rest in my roomy attics
pondering

black-holes, string
-theory, quasars, ethics,

plumbing your own depths
and mine too, perhaps.

Oh recumbent lodger
stuck in my gorge

and given the urge
to moan about the wallpaper,

that chaise-longue
like something in an Ottoman brothel,

like something on the lung.
Here, everyone's a pauper.

I hear your reedy voice
coughing up the heat-pipes

like some old codger
tubercular with vice.

Even if a cornball
moon peeps

upon my roof-slates
I know there's no respite.

So this is a NOTICE TO QUIT.
It states-

we have been together too long
and though it chokes

me to say it,
this tenancy is hereby revoked.

Colander Man

Butterflies. Both holding metal ingots to his lobes
    or etched in blue-black ink upon his skin,
wild markings of the lunar-moth
    writhe upon his shin
and ankles. What isn't tattooed
    is pierced, spiked, gelled or cropped
-a crop-circle appeared mysteriously one night
    in the back of his haircut-
tie-dyed, crimped or lopped,

not to mention the topiary of sideboards
    and goatee beard. No, not to mention them.
Yet the day came when all this came undone.
    When, like a prospector
panning for precious stones
    -s he spat out all the little bits of dirt
and fool's gold
    from his eyelids, nostrils, earlobes, lips
and chin even, yes, his foreskin,

-as once disported
    by the esteemed Prince Consort-
and they fell to the floor
    like pond-ripples, clinking
to leave him porous
    as if peppered with grapeshot from a blunderbuss.
(Skin-grafts meant that the butterflies
    had their day and that all the dyes
ran to the one colour and melted.)

Next, he discarded the buckles, bibs, straps,
    bull-dog clips and bullet-belts,
stepping out of the dropped hoop
    of his clothes -leaving them to the moths-
like a new-born thing.
    Then he ran outside to the breeze
and pavement-slap. Out amongst
    the colour-coded traffic.
The wind blew through him and made music.

My Luminous Daughter

Spins like a top
against the foliage on the projector.
The striped deckchair,
the striped lawn. Gnat-jitter.
    Sycamore shadow.

A fly crawling along a striped straw
to within an inch of sticky *Tizer.*
The slide-carousel is jamming, a ratcheted blur
   of Muybridge poses-

her toecap shunting the striped football
from the present to the past,
pre-foetus, post-foetus,
an X-ray shot of her delicate pelvic bones
    on a hospital lightbox.

A Mobius-strip of flypaper encrusted with beetles.

She kicks at the ball, misses, falls,
with a windmill flailing of arms,
her dress spreading like a speeded-up film
   of a flower unfolding.

Her mother's *Airmail* letter blooming in my fist.

Fallen Seraph

I died, knowingly, then cleverly followed my footsteps
back to familiar earth... loam marvellous
between my toes. My multiple surface abrasions
sutured back up again
of their own accord. The paparazzi
were goggled by white light.

Luxury is dangerous and the leisured
expendable. By the same token
rules are made to be obeyed or broken
though the ordinary still need them
and crowd at the gates. Me? I'm muzzy as a Meths-head
and my cough wouldn't harm a cobweb.

This waitress - is that what it is -?
hugs her own boredom with the nonchalance of a novice.
She should see heaven and all that hygienic
Formica. My entry was inimitable,
wafting A-line vapours, arriving on the pinhead
saying 'Budge over, boys' in my best Mae West.

This is a slight return. People move on the pavement
like fickle cells. Philosophers have said
that reality is an illusion and boy, are they way out.
This table is a table is a table
though somehow the drink I'm drinking,
     by miraculous osmosis
is igniting the top of that lime tree.

I shall drink more and illuminate the century.

The Hangover Dream
[Did His Hand On The Deck-rail Tremble?]

Like mine, now, on the glass,
    while my mind furrows against
the sound of machine-gun *Alka Seltzer.*
    I can't remember how this hangover
led to Hart Crane. Only that in dream
    he spat, high and hard
over the freezing deck-rail and his spit flew
    like a tiny bird, yet

when I try it lands upon my shoulder
    like some seedy epaulet.
But the pub had swayed beneath my feet
    exactly like the deck of *The Oriziba*
and the blur that was a girl
    had bent her lips to the candle,
had blown and all
    the accrued, liquid wax

in the scooped space beneath the wick
    had blown too
and speckled the wall,
    her elegant neck,
my mirror. Today it hardens
    to the patterns
of a stellar cluster. But she's gone and my eyes
    are laced with micro-dots

like some mad Seurat. I think in bits, recall
    that drunk in the book
-shop. 'Evening War. Evening War?
    George Bastard Sure? Montale?
John Clar — nah, John Updike,
    that's the guy — Rabbit something,
Rabbit Rich, Rabbit Rondeaux, Rab — '
    his voice trails off, into Spring, slow

-ly but calls back through the snow-swirls
of my *Alka-Seltzer.* 'So
how would you describe her
sigh towards the end? A screek? A moan?
That long
drawn-out cry
while your pearl-spots dried
or glistened?' The honour is mine. Ever

heard the wind through the wheatfields?
Ever heard the sea? Ever really listened?
-Hart Crane. Born Garretville, Ohio,
1889. Tried to build a bridge.
Didn't need to. Walked on water.-
Last night's notebooks
are filled with mysterious scrawl.
Did I make the leap?

Did my hand on the deck-rail tremble?

Yorick Says

Twenty-three years
under the *Astroturf*
is enough

to give anyone jaw-ache.
You lift me. Your
princely fingers find

three bowling-ball
holes. A receptacle
for your tears?

Once, I shouldered you
above the globe
and made a table roar

slick with a glib
jibe. But sanity is an ill
-ness of the mind

and I'm just a skull.
I can't contain your sadness,
only pour it.

I know I smell.
Want to hear
a joke?

No. Maybe not.
I'll keep my trap shut.
Let you say your bit.

Then hurl me into orbit,
knowing that
I'm your future.

Anon (A Life Story)

So stop to consider Mr Prolific himself -
oftwise scurrilous, oftwise bawdy,
but bashing it out all the same -
I speak of the slumped Anon,
replete with goose-feathered quill
taking his proud place within each century.
The dazzling array of styles
and multiple tones of voice-
even Shakespeare and Chaucer are outgunned
as he pens a schizophrenic villanelle.
Though his polymorphic diversity
obscures a balanced overview
he is always
a wow with publishers
due to the avoidance of royalties.
Squint hard
and you can almost see his face,

deep-pored, pitted with ennui.
His fingers flaking
to feathery on quills or keys.
Is it modesty
keeps him clinging to the ink-wet dark?
A translucent spectre
back-projected on History?
Or clubs and truncheons,
digital lists, a mailed fist
tattooing his oak-barred gate?
But They will always arrive too late,
him vanished through a trapdoor
in the damp, to find his smouldering insignia - @
and the date. All those wanted posters
panting
for a one-man pluralist
with a limp.

Anon : Coda

This is my last word on The State Of The Nation
now everything's made illegal.
Pigeons queuing up by King's Cross Station.
A rent-boy playing footsie with a bagel.

Ad Hoc Paradiso

Thus, leaving your scars
at the airport

you let all cares
depart,

learn to live with a typewriter
for a wife,

survive for weeks on water
and soixante-neuf,

map the daily
progress of the goatee,

dally
under the ubiquitous oak tree,

read *After The Fall,*
inhale

the pastoral
and swig from The Holy Grail.

Let the mossy mailbox become God,
worship white envelopes,

(brown ones bring no good)
jump stiles, make associative leaps,

spurn
all offers and ex-wives,

spawn
children,

let them break upon
the addled lawn

like waves, like waves
unencumbered by the painful

convex rainfall
that gathers over Mount_____,

begin to count sheep or *Nembutal,*
lose count,

pray for the lost hitcher,
who, arriving by courtesy of thunderstorm

with her rucksack of allusion
inhabits your guest room

to fulfil the role
of prospective biographer

to chronicle
what critics

will
later call

your
'relatively undocumented year

of rustic
seclusion'.

The Masters And The Trees

Perhaps they owed it to each other,
these homages, these sinuous tributes.
Firstly, I see the trees, great shimmer
-ings, reaching out to an immediate neighbour

and light, like a vine, clambering up to the open parachutes
above. And secondly, them-
scratching in swollen notebooks for a theme
to gather the sap of themselves

into an enervating law. The flaw being that nothing
could solve
the discrepancy between the vision and the thing

itself: the treeness of a tree
or the wordiness of words. So, noting
birds on the brink of both, they became birds.

Matthew Caley's work has appeared in six small press collections, the most recent being *Sirens [The Brixton Soundtrack]* from Slow Dancer. He has given many readings, been published in numerous periodicals and anthologies and his work has been broadcast on BBC Radio 4. His is also involved in an on-going collaboration with artist Stephen Nicholas and their work has been seen in a series of exhibitions both here and abroad. He lives and writes in London.

Thirst is his first full-length collection.